PUFFIN BOOKS

Not Quite a Mermaid
MERMAID RESCUE

...shire with
...tain dogs.
...s her time
...horse

Books by Linda Chapman

MY SECRET UNICORN series
STARDUST series
NOT QUITE A MERMAID series

BRIGHT LIGHTS
CENTRE STAGE

Not Quite a Mermaid

MERMAID RESCUE

LINDA CHAPMAN

Illustrated by Dawn Apperley

PUFFIN

PUFFIN BOOKS

Published by the Penguin Group
Penguin Books Ltd, 80 Strand, London WC2R 0RL, England
Penguin Group (USA) Inc., 375 Hudson Street, New York, New York 10014, USA
Penguin Group (Canada), 90 Eglinton Avenue East, Suite 700, Toronto, Ontario,
Canada M4P 2Y3 (a division of Pearson Penguin Canada Inc.)
Penguin Ireland, 25 St Stephen's Green, Dublin 2, Ireland
(a division of Penguin Books Ltd)
Penguin Group (Australia), 250 Camberwell Road, Camberwell, Victoria 3124, Australia
(a division of Pearson Australia Group Pty Ltd)
Penguin Books India Pvt Ltd, 11 Community Centre, Panchsheel Park,
New Delhi – 110 017, India
Penguin Group (NZ), 67 Apollo Drive, Rosedale, North Shore 0632, New Zealand
(a division of Pearson New Zealand Ltd)
Penguin Books (South Africa) (Pty) Ltd, 24 Sturdee Avenue, Rosebank,
Johannesburg 2196, South Africa

Penguin Books Ltd, Registered Offices: 80 Strand, London WC2R 0RL, England

puffinbooks.com

First published 2008
1

Text copyright © Linda Chapman, 2008
Illustrations copyright © Dawn Apperley, 2008
All rights reserved

The moral right of the author and illustrator has been asserted

Set in Palatino 15/27 pt
Typeset by Palimpsest Book Production Limited, Grangemouth, Stirlingshire
Made and printed in England by Clays Ltd, St Ives plc

British Library Cataloguing in Publication Data
A CIP catalogue record for this book is available from the British Library

ISBN: 978-0-141-32231-5

lindachapman.co.uk

www.greenpenguin.co.uk

Penguin Books is committed to a sustainable future
for our business, our readers and our planet.
The book in your hands is made from paper
certified by the Forest Stewardship Council.

To Maya Gardman

Contents

Chapter One

'Quick, Splash! Let's hide!' Electra the mermaid dived into an enormous blue basket sponge. She ducked inside its hollow middle while Splash, her pet dolphin, hid behind it.

'Electra! Splash!' Electra heard Keri

and Marina, her two friends, calling.

'BOO!' Electra and Splash cried, jumping out together just as Marina and Keri swam past.

The two mermaids squealed and shot up through the water in surprise.

'Made you jump!' Electra said in delight. She loved playing tricks on people.

'Electra!' Marina threw a handful of slimy seaweed at her.

Electra ducked and giggled. 'What shall we do now?'

It was Marina's birthday and the three of them and Splash had come to Craggy Island with Marina's parents for the afternoon. Craggy Island was across the deep sea from Mermaid Island where all the merpeople lived. The merpeople didn't usually visit it because they weren't keen on swimming across the deep sea but Marina had persuaded her parents that it was where she really wanted to go for her birthday. The girls and Splash had eaten the birthday picnic with Marina's parents and now they were exploring the island on their own.

'We could go into the sea forest,' Marina suggested, looking to the right where there was a thick forest of sea firs leading out into the sea. 'Or we could keep going round the island and see what else we can find.'

'Let's keep going round,' said Keri. 'There might be some caves or deep sea potholes to explore.'

'Yes!' Electra's eyes shone. 'We might find weird sea creatures we've never seen before.'

Most of the merchildren didn't like doing anything that might be even the slightest bit scary but Electra loved doing exciting things. That was why she liked playing with Marina and Keri. They were two years older than her and they loved having adventures too.

Just then a shoal of tiny blue damselfish swept past them. 'Come on!' cried Marina. 'Let's swim with the fish!'

The three mermaids and Splash dived among the shoal and let themselves be swept along. Electra grabbed Splash's fin. She wasn't as fast as the others because she had legs

and feet instead of a tail. Electra had been born a human. The merpeople had found her floating alone in a boat after a big storm when she had been just a tiny baby. They had given her sea powder so she could breathe underwater and Maris, a young mermaid who didn't have any children, had adopted her. Electra couldn't imagine living a human life now. She loved being a mermaid!

'Wheee!' she cried as the damselfish swooped up and down. It was an amazing feeling to be surrounded by the shimmering, sparkling shoal. She could hear a constant faint buzzing noise. She knew it was the fish talking to each other. Electra had just started learning how to talk fish language at school. She loved it but so far she had only practised talking to big fish; talking to lots of little ones was much more difficult because they all spoke at the same time! For her half-term holiday homework, she had to talk to a fish and write about its life. *I think I'll choose bigger fish than these*, she thought as the tiny damselfish chatted and whispered all around her.

The shoal of fish suddenly swooped upwards, leaving Electra and her friends alone in the clear turquoise water.

'That was fun!' Electra said breathlessly. She looked around and spotted something strange. Near to where they had stopped was a very white, odd-looking coral reef. 'Look at that!' she said curiously, swimming towards it with Splash. 'I've never seen coral that white before.'

As she got closer she caught her breath. The reason the coral was such a strange white colour was that it was dead. All the bright living bits of it had been eaten away by something, leaving just a bare skeleton.

'What's happened to it?' Splash asked.

'I don't know,' Electra replied. She stared at the coral; it looked horrible – very still and ghostly with large holes in bits of the reef. No fish were swimming through it. It stretched on and on. Splash moved closer to Electra's side.

'It's been eaten by a gang of Crown of Thorns starfish,' Keri said as she and Marina joined Electra.

Electra frowned. 'What?'

Keri shuddered. 'Crown of Thorns starfish are big red starfish who destroy coral.'

'They arrive in groups and eat all the living bits, killing the reef and leaving it like this,' said Marina.

'They're really scary,' Keri added. 'They've got poisonous spikes all over them. Grown-up merpeople can sweep them back out to sea using wave magic but otherwise the only things that can get rid of them are giant sea snails or a few of the bigger fish who like eating them.'

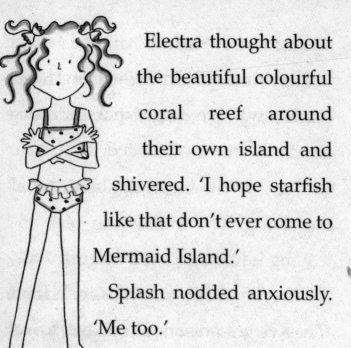

Electra thought about the beautiful colourful coral reef around their own island and shivered. 'I hope starfish like that don't ever come to Mermaid Island.'

Splash nodded anxiously. 'Me too.'

'Come on, let's get away from here,' said Marina, backing away from the creepy reef.

They swam on and soon came to a pretty cove. As they popped up through the surface of the water they saw a beach with glittering white sands and five large rocks sticking out of the sea that looked perfect for sitting on. 'Let's stop here,' said Marina.

They swam to the largest rock. Electra climbed right to the top. Marina and Keri each found a ledge lower down to sit on where their tails could dangle into the cool water. Splash swam round them.

Electra glanced down. She could see all the way to the sandy seabed. There was a circle of rocks and some mounds of seaweed that almost looked like four beds. An idea suddenly popped into her head. 'Hey! Wouldn't this be a brilliant place to come camping? We could use the seaweed down there as our beds and make a campfire with mermaid fire in the circle of stones!'

'Oh, wow!' exclaimed Keri. 'That's a great idea, Electra! We could bring our own food to cook.'

'Yeah! We could sleep in sleeping bags with no grown-ups around,' said Marina.

'And have a midnight feast!' said

Splash. 'It would be such an adventure!'

'It would.' Electra looked at them, her eyes shining. 'Let's ask our parents straight away!'

Chapter Two

'I really hope Mum says we can go camping,' Electra said to Splash as they swam home later that afternoon. Marina's parents had agreed to the camping trip and Keri was sure her parents would say yes too.

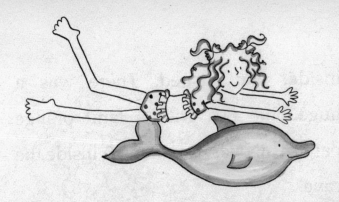

'It would be so much fun!' said Splash.

'We'll ask as soon as we get home!' Electra decided.

'We'd better get a move on,' Splash reminded her. 'You know your mum said not to be late today.'

They swam swiftly through the water, taking the short cut past the deepest caves in the reef. As they swam past one cave, Electra glanced inside. She gasped. There was a huge blue fish with a faint orange pattern all over it swimming inside the cave.

'Look, Splash!' she whispered.

The fish was almost as big as a shark. It had orange eyes, a large rounded forehead and enormous blue lips. It turned and saw them. For a moment, Electra wondered whether they should swim away as fast as they could but she decided that actually it didn't look very fierce. It blinked curiously at them. Electra tried to remember everything she had learnt about speaking fish language at school. 'Hello,' she said. Speaking fish language was a bit strange because you had to make your mouth round like a fish's and let the words bubble out of you.

'Hello, little mermaid,' the fish replied in a deep voice. He looked rather uncertainly at her legs. 'You *are* a mermaid, aren't you?'

'Oh, yes.' Electra smiled at him. 'My name's Electra and this is my dolphin, Splash.' Electra edged closer. The big fish seemed friendly enough even though it was enormous. 'What's your name and what type of fish are you?'

'My name is Kai,' the fish replied. 'I am a Napoleon fish.'

'Do you live here?' Electra asked curiously, wondering why she hadn't ever seen him before.

Kai nodded. 'I have just moved in. Humans kept

coming to the island that my friends and I were living near and we decided we needed a new place to stay. We were swimming past your island when the mermen guarding the gate called to us and said we could come and live in the caves here.'

A hundred questions bubbled up in Electra's mind – what did Kai and his friends eat? What did they like to do? How old were they? Suddenly she remembered her homework project. Kai would be the perfect fish to interview! 'I have to do a project on a fish for school,' she said quickly.

'Could I do it on you, please? It would just mean asking you some questions and maybe drawing a picture of you.'

'Of course,' said Kai. 'Ask away.'

But before Electra could start, Splash nudged her. 'You'd better not ask questions now, Electra. We're going to be really late!'

Electra realized he was right. 'I've got to go home now but can I come back and talk to you another time, please, Kai?'

The big fish nodded easily. 'Any time, little mermaid.'

'See you soon then!' Electra said. 'Bye!'

She and Splash hastily dived away.

Despite not having talked for long to Kai, they got home twenty minutes late. Maris was waiting in the cave entrance, coughing and glancing around anxiously. She looked relieved when she saw Electra and Splash. 'Where have you two been? It's twenty past five.'

'Sorry, Mum,' said Electra quickly. 'It's just I saw this fish and –'

'You saw a fish! Oh, Electra!' Maris interrupted crossly. She sneezed. 'I've been really worried about you. I thought something must have happened on Craggy Island or out in the deep sea. You know I told you both to come straight home today. Honestly!' Turning round she swam into the cave, coughing.

Electra looked at Splash.

'Oh dear, Mum's not in a very good mood, is she?'

He shook his head. 'Maybe it's her cold.' Maris was usually very cheerful but she'd had a bad cold for the last few days and judging from the sneezes they could hear coming from inside the cave it was getting worse and not better.

Electra and Splash went into the cave. Maris had gone into the kitchen.

'When are we going to ask her about the camping trip?' Splash said. 'I want to find out if we can go!' He whizzed around the cave in excitement. 'Just think about it, Electra! A campfire!' He gave a flick of his tail. 'A midnight feast!' He gave another flick. 'Sleeping outside!'

'Watch out!' Electra cried as Splash's tail caught a glass bowl that was on top of a low table. It smashed down on to the floor. Shards of glass flew everywhere.

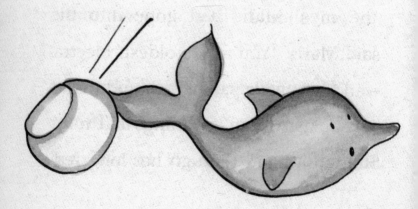

'Whoops,' said Splash, stopping dead.

'What was that noise?' Maris swam quickly out of the kitchen. She broke off with a gasp. 'Oh, no!'

'Sorry, Maris,' Splash said sheepishly.

'He didn't mean to do it, Mum,' said Electra. 'He was just swimming too fast.'

'You should have stopped him!' said Maris. 'You're the oldest, Electra – and he's your pet. You should make sure Splash doesn't do things like that.' She ran a hand through her long red hair. 'First being late and now this! I wish you could be more responsible.'

'It wasn't Electra's fault,' Splash said quickly. 'Please don't be cross with her, Maris. I shouldn't have been swimming that fast inside. I was just excited.'

'Why?' Maris asked him.

Electra was sure that now was *not* a good time to ask her mum about the trip. She shook her head frantically at Splash but he didn't see her.

'Electra and I want to go camping on Craggy Island with Marina and Keri in two days' time,' he said eagerly, swimming over to Maris and looking at her hopefully. 'Marina's mum and dad have said she can go and Keri is sure her mum will say yes. Can Electra and I go as well, Maris?'

Electra held her breath. What would her mum say?

Maris shook her head. 'No, I'm afraid not. You're not old enough to go camping on Craggy Island.'

'But Marina and Keri are going,' protested Electra.

'They're two years older than you, Electra,' Maris pointed out. 'You're not grown up or sensible enough. You'll get into trouble.'

'I won't!' Electra exclaimed.

'No, Electra. My mind's made up.' Maris rubbed a hand over her head and groaned slightly. 'Look, I've got a headache. I'm going to go and lie down for a little while.'

She swam into her bedroom.

Electra stared after her. 'We can't go camping,' she said slowly. Tears welled in her eyes. She had really, really been looking forward to it. She'd thought her mum might take some persuading but she hadn't thought she would just say a definite no.

Splash nuzzled her. 'Maybe your mum will change her mind,' he said. 'Perhaps she'll feel better after a rest.'

Electra bit her lip. She hoped so.

Chapter Three

Maris didn't change her mind about the camping trip. After her rest, she still said they couldn't go. Electra and Splash ate their supper in gloomy silence. Pictures of the campsite at Craggy Island kept flashing through Electra's mind.

She pushed the sea cabbage around on her plate. *One minute Mum's telling me I should be more grown up and responsible, and the next she's saying I'm too young to go camping*, she thought. *It's not fair!*

Across the table, Maris sneezed and coughed.

The next morning, Electra and Splash set out to Marina's cave to tell her the bad news. When they got there they found Marina and Keri sitting in the lounge with paper and pens.

'Hi!' Marina said eagerly to them. 'You're just in time. We were about to start making a list of all the things we'll need to take with us when we go camping tomorrow.'

'We can't come,' Electra said. 'My mum said no.'

Marina and Keri's faces fell. 'Oh,' said Marina.

Electra sighed and sat down on the sofa. 'She says we're not old enough.'

Keri looked at her sympathetically.

'Never mind. Maybe we'll be able to go again next year and she'll let you come then.'

Electra nodded glumly. It was kind of Keri to try and cheer her up but next year felt like a very long way away. She wanted to go camping now!

Electra and Splash didn't stay at Marina's for very long. Electra felt left out as she listened to her friends planning their trip – talking about what they should pack and what they needed to take with them.

'What should we do now?' asked

Splash as he and Electra swam away.

'Why don't we go and see that Napoleon fish again?' Electra suggested, shifting her mermaid bag on her shoulder. 'I can interview him for my school project. I've got paper and a pen in my bag.'

They went down to the caves where they had seen the fish the day before. He wasn't there. Electra went into the cave. 'Where's he gone?'

Suddenly she spotted Kai, the big fish, lying underneath a stony ledge. 'Oh, there he is! He's asleep,' she whispered. 'We'd better leave him, Splash.'

Kai opened one eye. 'Hello, little mermaid,' he said in his slow voice, bubbles coming out of his mouth.

'I'm sorry, we didn't mean to disturb you,' Electra said in fish language.

'That's all right.' With a flick of his

tail, Kai swam out from under the ledge. He looked into her face with his orange eye, his huge lips opening and closing as he used his fins to hover in the water beside her. 'So, would you like to ask me some questions for your homework project, little mermaid?'

'Yes, please! How old are you? What do you eat? What do you like doing?' The questions burst out of Electra. She had so much she wanted to ask him!

'I'm twenty years old,' said Kai, taking a deep breath. 'I eat clams and crabs, spiny fish, starfish and sea urchins – my lips are tough so their prickles don't hurt me. I like living in caves and I go out early in the morning to look for food. I've got five friends. We all live in our own caves.'

Electra took some paper and a pencil out of her bag. 'Please can I write some of this down and draw a picture of you so that I can show my teacher?'

'Of course,' Kai smiled. As Electra began to write and draw, he talked more about his life. His favourite food was spiky starfish and he showed Electra how he could blow powerful jets of water out of his mouth to blast away sand if he thought tasty creatures might be hiding there.

Electra finished her drawing. 'Thank you for talking to us,' she said politely.

Kai pushed his head against her hand. 'My pleasure.' He opened his mouth extra wide almost as if he was yawning. 'Now, I think I'll carry on with my nap.'

'Bye!' Electra and Splash called. They headed out of the cave.

'I bet no one else at school talks to a Napoleon fish for *their* project!' said Electra, so delighted by the thought that she almost forgot about her disappointment at not being able to go on the camping trip. 'I'll write everything he said down properly when we get home.'

Splash nudged her. 'Can we play a game now?'

'Yes!' Electra tagged him before darting away. 'Let's play tag! You're it!'

Splash raced after her and laughing and shouting the two of them took it in turns to chase each other through the coral reef.

When they got back to their cave, Electra settled down to write up her school project. Just as she was finishing, Maris arrived home, carrying four heavy shopping bags. Her nose was red and she was coughing as she came into the cave. She looked very tired.

'Hi, Mum!' Electra said.

'Hello.' Maris put the bags down with a sigh and sneezed. 'Oh, this cold, I wish it would go away.'

'Why don't you take some sea moss?' Electra asked her. Sea moss grew near the deep caves. It was very good for colds.

'We've run out,' Maris replied. 'If my cold's no better tomorrow I'll have to go and get some. But I just don't feel like swimming all the way to the deep caves at the moment. So, what have you two been doing?'

'We went to see Marina and Keri first of all and then we saw a Napoleon fish and I interviewed him for my school project.' Electra held up her homework. 'Look! I've just finished it, Mum.'

'Well done,' her mum said, looking surprised. 'I'll have a look at it later.' She coughed. 'But I think I'd better go and have a lie down right now. I'm really not feeling well.' She swam into the bedroom.

'Oh dear, your mum does look ill,' said Splash.

Electra felt worried. 'I wish we had some sea moss that she could take.'

'Couldn't we go and get some for her?' Splash asked.

Electra stared at him. That was a great idea! 'Of course we could! It's too late now – she won't let us go to the deep caves when it's getting dark

– but we could get up early and go and pick some first thing.'

'I know! We could make your mum breakfast in bed and take her the sea moss at the same time to make her feel better,' said Splash.

Electra grinned at him. 'OK! Let's do it!'

Chapter Four

Electra and Splash got up as soon as the sun rose the next morning. Electra put on her rucksack. She would put the sea moss in it. 'We'd better hurry,' she whispered to Splash as they swam out of the cave. 'We need to be back before Mum wakes up or she'll get worried.'

They hurried towards the deep caves. There had been a storm in the night and bits of seaweed and driftwood were floating through the water. Electra had heard her mum swimming around in the night making sure the door and windows of the cave were shut. She hoped that it meant her mum would sleep in that morning and not wake up before they were back.

Electra shifted the rucksack into a more comfortable position on her back and thought about Marina and Keri.

They'd be setting off on their camping trip at lunchtime. *I wish I was going with them,* she thought with a sigh. She would have loved to have been packing her rucksack with camping things and getting ready to go.

She and Splash dived down through the turquoise water. As they passed Kai's cave, Electra checked to see if the Napoleon fish was inside but he wasn't. For a moment she wondered where he was but then she remembered what he'd said about how he usually hunted for food first thing in the morning. He must be out getting his breakfast!

'Do you know where the sea moss grows?' Splash asked her.

'I'm sure I can remember seeing some near where the hole is in the coral wall,' Electra replied.

No one else knew about the hole in the wall. It wasn't very big – only just big enough for Electra to squeeze through – and it was usually covered by a curtain of seaweed. She climbed through the hole when she wanted to get into the deep sea without anyone knowing.

They swam on and found the hole. It was easy to spot that day. The storm in the night had ripped the seaweed away and some of the coral around the edges had broken off in the storm. Now the hole was big enough for even Splash's round tummy to fit through.

'Oh dear. The storm's made it much bigger,' Splash said.

'We should tell someone about it,' Electra said. She didn't want to. She liked having a secret way into the deep sea but she knew it was too dangerous to have a hole that big in the wall. A shark or some other dangerous creature might swim through it. 'We'd better tell Mum when we get home, but first let's get the sea moss. Look! There it is!'

Some nearby rocks were covered with a short purple moss. Electra began to pull up handfuls. It tore away easily. Splash helped, tugging the moss up with his mouth. They stuffed it into her rucksack.

'Your mum's going to be so pleased!' said Splash happily.

'Especially if we can get back in time to make her breakfast in bed as well,' said Electra. 'We've got loads of moss now. Come on, let's get home.'

But just as they turned and began to swim past the hole they heard a strange noise coming from the other side of the coral wall – a crunching, chomping type of noise.

'What's that?' wondered Splash.

Electra listened. It sounded like a creature munching on something hard – but not just one creature eating, she realized, lots of creatures. 'I don't know what it is,' she said curiously. 'Should we go and see?'

Splash looked uncertain. 'What if it's something dangerous?'

Electra knew they probably should go straight home but she'd never heard anything like that noise and she really wanted to know what it was!

'Let's just have a quick look,' she said.

They swam through the hole. Electra gasped. 'Splash! Look!'

A gang of about a hundred red

starfish was swarming over the outside of the reef wall. Each starfish was as about half as long as Electra's arm and they were covered in long poisonous spines. To Electra's horror, she saw that they were eating their way through the beautiful pink and purple coral wall, reducing it to a white skeleton as they gobbled up all the colourful living bits.

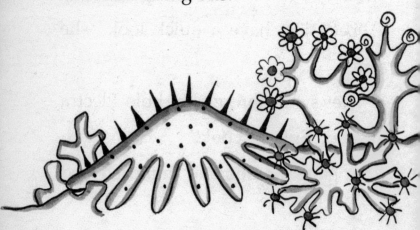

'Crown of Thorns starfish!' Electra gasped, remembering what Marina and Keri had told her.

'The storm must have swept them here,' said Splash in alarm. 'They're destroying the coral. What are we going to do? If they eat through the wall the island won't be safe any more!'

'We'd better get help!' Electra cried. 'And fast!'

Chapter Five

Electra and Splash dived back through the hole in the wall. 'Let's go and tell the guards on the gates. Do you remember that Marina said adult merpeople can use wave magic to sweep the starfish away,' Electra said, swimming as fast as she could.

'That's going to take ages! The gate's all the way round the other side of the island,' Splash said anxiously. 'And the starfish are eating the coral so quickly. They're going to really damage it!'

'Well, what else can we do?' Electra asked as they swooshed past the deep caves. 'Unless . . . Yes!' An idea exploded into her brain. 'Kai! He said his favourite food was spiky starfish. Hang on! Stop, Splash!'

They screeched to a stop beside

Kai's cave. Electra swam to the entrance. 'Kai! Kai!' she shouted in fish language. Her heart pounded. Her plan would only work if the big fish was there.

To her relief, Kai was back from hunting for his breakfast and he came swimming to the entrance of the cave. 'Hello, little mermaid,' he said curiously. 'This is an early morning visit.'

'It's not just a visit!' Electra told him desperately. 'We need your help, Kai. There's about a hundred Crown of Thorns starfish on the other side of the coral wall and they're eating it up!'

Kai's orange eyes widened. 'Crown of Thorns starfish! They're nasty vicious creatures – but very tasty!'

'We have to stop them,' Electra said. 'If they damage the wall too much Mermaid Island won't be a safe place to live any more. Can you help us? *Please!'*

Kai looked worried. 'I would. The merpeople have been very kind to us. I would hate to see your reef damaged but I'm full up at the moment. I've just had my breakfast.'

'You don't have to eat them!' said Splash, swimming up beside Electra. 'You could just chase them away.'

'Yes!' said Electra. 'I bet they'll be scared of you, Kai. Maybe if they see you coming they'll swim away and leave the reef alone.'

Kai smiled. 'Count me in. I'll see if my friends will help too.'

He swooshed out of his cave and into the surrounding ones. Soon there were six Napoleon fish all swimming around, their big mouths opening and closing.

'Everyone wants to help you!' said Kai. 'Just show us the way!'

Electra grabbed Splash's fin and he zoomed off through the water towards the hole. It was just big enough for the Napoleon fish to fit through.

'This way!' called Splash.

The big fish raced after him. 'They're just over there!' Electra cried. Even as she spoke the Napoleon fish saw the spiky starfish. 'Attack! Attack!' cried Kai.

All six fish swam towards the reef wall. Seeing them, the starfish suddenly began to panic. Their munching stopped abruptly and they scrambled over each other, trying to get out of the way of the fish.

The Napoleon fish were all too full to want to eat any of the starfish but the spiky creatures didn't realize that. They began to jump off the reef, abandoning their coral meal.

Kai grabbed the biggest one in his mouth and tossed it out into the sea. His friends joined in. Soon the water was full of flying starfish. The ones that weren't grabbed by the Napoleon fish swam frantically after their friends. The big fish chased after them, bumping them along with their noses and bouncing them through the water.

'Yippee!' whistled Splash, clapping his flippers as the starfish fled from the reef.

'Hurray!' shouted Electra.

'Electra, watch out!' cried Splash in alarm as a stray starfish swam straight towards her, its spines long and dangerous. Electra gasped and tried to swim out of the way but it was too late. It was going to get her! It put its spines out and zoomed faster, straight at her legs!

Just in time, Kai saw what was happening. He swooped down and shot a blast of water at the starfish. The water knocked it off course. It somersaulted through the water, a surprised expression on its face.

'Leave my little mermaid friend alone!' Kai charged towards it. The starfish fled after the others with the fish in hot pursuit.

'They've gone!' said Splash as Kai returned and the other five Napoleon fish swam up. Electra looked. Splash was right. The reef was now clear. Some of the coral had been damaged but Electra was relieved to see that most of it was still fine. She shivered as she thought what the reef might have looked like if Kai and his friends *hadn't* been there to help.

'Thank you so much,' she said to all the Napoleon fish. 'You've saved the coral!'

'Our pleasure,' said Kai, looking as if he'd enjoyed himself. 'It was fun!'

'Should we go and chase them some more?' said one of his friends, his eyes sparkling.

The others nodded eagerly. 'We don't want them to think about coming back,' said another.

Electra grinned as they set off. She had a feeling the horrible Crown of Thorns starfish wouldn't come near Mermaid Island *ever* again! 'Come on.

We'd better get home,' she said to Splash.

A voice behind her made her jump. 'Electra! Whatever are you doing?'

Electra swung round. Her mum was standing on the other side of the hole, looking very cross indeed!

Chapter Six

'Mum!' Electra said in shock.

'Whatever are you doing?' Maris exclaimed. 'I woke up and found that you and Splash had gone. What are you doing out here in the deep sea?' Her eyes fell on the rucksack on

Electra's back. 'And why have you got your rucksack?' Her eyes widened. 'Oh, Electra, you weren't trying to sneak off and go camping, were you?'

'No!' Electra exclaimed in horror. 'I was –'

'Come back through the wall this instant!' Maris snapped, breaking off to cough. 'I'm very disappointed in you.'

'But I wasn't about to sneak off. Really I wasn't,' Electra said, swimming towards her.

'No,' said Splash quickly. 'We were –'

'I'm just as cross with you as well, Splash,' Maris interrupted. 'You should both know better. I said you weren't allowed to go! I said –'

'But, Mum, we weren't trying to go camping!' Electra shouted in exasperation. She reached into her bag. 'We came here to get this!' Pulling out a handful of sea moss, she held it up.

Her mum fell silent and stared at it. 'Sea moss?'

'Yes, for you. To make your cold better,' said Electra, lowering her voice. 'We knew you felt too ill to come and get some.'

'We were going to bring you breakfast in bed as well,' Splash said.

Maris suddenly looked like she didn't know what to say. 'Oh.'

'We weren't sneaking off to go camping, Mum,' Electra said. 'We just didn't want you to feel ill any more.'

Maris sighed. 'I'm sorry,' she said. 'I saw the rucksack and you both in the deep sea and I just jumped to the wrong conclusion.' She swam forwards and hugged them. 'It was a lovely thought. Thank you. I'm sorry I shouted at you when you were being so kind and just trying to help.'

'It was lucky we *were* here,' said Splash, looking up at her. 'Because when we were getting the moss we heard a noise through the wall. We went to see what it was –'

'And found about a hundred Crown

of Thorns starfish eating the coral,' finished Electra.

Maris looked alarmed. 'Crown of Thorns starfish! We'd better get help. They'll destroy the wall!'

'Wait, Mum!' said Electra quickly as Maris turned to swim off. 'We've already got rid of them.'

Maris looked at her in astonishment. 'You've got rid of them? But how?'

Before Electra could reply, Kai and his friends came swimming back.

Maris gasped as she saw the six huge Napoleon fish.

'Hi, Kai,' said Electra.

'All the starfish have gone,' he told her.

'Thank you,' Electra said. She saw him look curiously at Maris.

'This is my mum,' Electra told him. 'Mum, this is Kai, the Napoleon fish who I talked to for my school project. He told me then that he liked eating spiny creatures so when I saw the starfish I asked him to help. He and his friends chased the starfish away. It was quicker than swimming to tell the guards on the gate.'

'And it was our pleasure,' Kai said to Maris. 'Chasing spiny starfish is almost as much fun as eating them!' He opened his mouth and blew a bubble. 'It was very quick thinking from Electra to have the idea of asking me to help with the starfish. You must be very proud of her.'

'Oh, I am.' Maris smiled at Electra. 'I really am.'

Electra felt a rush of relief. It looked like she wasn't in trouble any more!

'So, Splash and I did the right thing?' she asked her mum.

Maris nodded. 'Just the right thing. There would have been a lot more damage done to the reef if you hadn't thought of asking Kai for help. Well done. You too, Splash.'

Splash whistled happily.

Kai turned to Electra. 'Goodbye, little mermaid. Do come and visit me again soon.'

'I will,' Electra promised. Kai and his friends swam away.

Maris watched them go and shook her head. 'Oh, Electra. What will you get up to next?'

Electra grinned at her. 'I hope it's something exciting, whatever it is!'

Maris hesitated for a moment. 'Would a camping trip count as exciting?'

Electra frowned. What did her mum mean?

'Do you both still want to go camping with Marina and Keri today?' Maris asked.

'Yes!' Splash and Electra exclaimed.

'Then you can go!' A broad smile lit up Maris's face. 'I was obviously wrong to say you weren't grown up enough. You've both been very responsible and sensible. And after everything you've done this morning, you deserve a holiday treat. Splash, why don't you whizz round to Marina's house and tell her parents I've said that you and Electra can come too? Tell them you and Electra will meet them at the gate at lunchtime. Electra, you and I can go and pack everything you and Splash will need.'

'Including a midnight feast?' Electra said hopefully.

Maris smiled at her. 'Oh yes – the biggest midnight feast you can carry!'

The news soon spread about Electra and Splash having got rid of the Crown of Thorns starfish. All morning people called in to congratulate them on their quick thinking. Maris made herself some sea moss medicine and was soon feeling better.

'Have a great time!' she told them as Electra put her rucksack on ready to go camping.

Electra hugged her. 'We will.'

Splash nuzzled Maris. 'We'll see you tomorrow.'

'Bye!' Maris called, waving them off.

Electra grabbed hold of Splash's fin. 'Come on, Splash! Let's go!'

Electra and Splash met Marina and Keri and Marina's parents at the gates and they all swam over to Craggy

Island together. The girls and Splash took their camping things to the cove they had seen on their last visit, and Marina's mum and dad set out their own camping things in the next cove along so that they would be there if the girls and Splash needed them but out of sight for most of the time.

'Isn't this fun?' said Marina as they made beds out of the seaweed and put their sleeping bags on top. 'It's like being here all on our own!'

'We can make a fire and cook our tea,' said Keri, taking out a box full of seaweed sausages.

'Mum and Dad have given me some sea mallows to toast,' said Marina.

'And I've got a midnight feast,' said Electra, pulling out the box she had packed with her mum. It was crammed with cakes and sweets.

Splash blew out a bubble happily. 'I think I'm going to like camping!'

They gathered some magic mermaid fire from the bottom of the sea and cooked their seaweed sausages and then they toasted their sea mallows on long sticks and told ghost stories. Finally they curled up in their sleeping bags around the fire and shared out their midnight feast.

Marina fell asleep first and then Keri.

Electra shared her last pink sugar starfish with Splash and sighed happily as they watched the flames of the campfire. 'It's been a brilliant day, hasn't it?'

Splash nodded and yawned sleepily. 'I wonder what our next adventure will be.'

Electra snuggled down beside him. 'I don't know.' She grinned at him. 'But I bet it'll be something fun!'

Discover magical new worlds with

Linda Chapman

The Circle of
Secrets & Magic
lindachapman.co.uk

⭐ **Gallop** with the unicorns at Unicorn Meadows

⭐ **Fly** with the magical spirits of Stardust Forest

⭐ **Swim** through Mermaid Falls with Electra and her friends

⭐ **Play** with new friends at Unicorn School

With great **activities**, gorgeous **downloads**, games galore and an exciting new online fanzine!

What are you waiting for?
The magic begins at

lindachapman.co.uk